# Doug's Bugs

## Contents

T0337138

Written by Jane Clarke

Illustrated by Esther P Cuadrado

**Collins**

# What's in this story?

Listen and say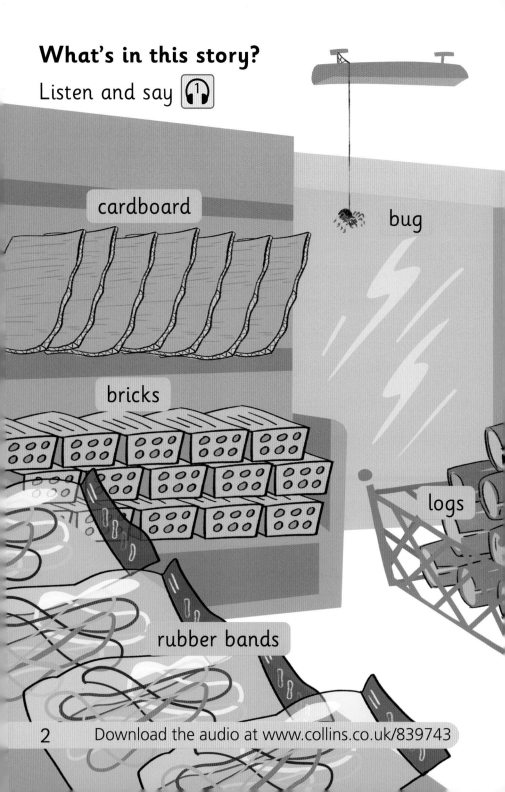

cardboard

bug

bricks

logs

rubber bands

Download the audio at www.collins.co.uk/839743

flowerpots

plastic bottles

jam jars

## Chapter 1 A bug in the bath!

Doug was in his bedroom. Doug loved **bugs**.
His favourite book was his *Big Book of Bugs*.

One page in his book was about a beetle.
It was big and black and it had six legs.
Doug liked beetles.

Doug wanted a beetle. He wanted it to live in a **tank** in his room. But his sister Sally was **scared** of beetles. Sally didn't like bugs!

beetle

Eek!

Sally was in the bathroom. She saw a bug in the bath. She called Doug.

Doug looked at the bug. It was a small ladybird.

"I don't like it!" said Sally.

"Don't worry," Doug said. "I can put it in a tank!"

 ladybird

Doug didn't have a tank, so he found a clean jam **jar**, some kitchen paper and a **rubber band**.

Now Doug had a pet ladybird in a jam jar! His pet needed something to drink, so he put water in an old bottle top and gave it to his ladybird.

It needed something to eat, too. He knew ladybirds liked eating aphids.

aphid

Doug's ladybird couldn't eat aphids in the jar. So Doug put his ladybird on the floor. Then it could find aphids in his room.

## Chapter 2 The second bug

That afternoon, Sally found a bug in some flowers.

"*Eek!* I don't like bugs!" said Sally.

Doug looked at the bug. It was a small caterpillar.

"Don't worry," said Doug. "I can put it in a jam jar."

caterpillar

Doug put the caterpillar in a jam jar. He gave it a leaf to eat. Now he had two jam jars and two pet bugs in his room. Doug was happy.

Doug's bedroom was next to Sally's room and his sister was not happy.

She said, "I don't want your bugs in our house!"

Doug was **worried**. His bugs were not safe in his bedroom. He needed to find them a safe place to live. Where could they go?

Doug looked at his *Big Book of Bugs*. It had lots of ideas. Then he saw the best idea. His bugs could live in a **bug hotel**!

# Chapter 3 The bug hotel

Doug needed lots of things to make a
bug hotel. He looked in the **recycling bin**
and found a **plastic bottle**, an old **flowerpot**
and some **cardboard**.

There were some good things in the garden, too. Doug found five **bricks**, three **logs** and some rocks. Then he found some leaves, some sticks and some long, dry grass.

He put everything next to the **pond**.

Doug put the rocks, the bottle, the flowerpot, the sticks and the logs on the bricks. He put the leaves and the dry grass on, too.

16

Doug looked at his bug hotel. There were lots of places for bugs to hide from the weather. It was dry and they had water to drink. There were plants to eat, too.

## Chapter 4 A change

Doug went to his bedroom. He looked at the jam jar with the caterpillar in it. But the caterpillar was now a different shape.

Doug looked in his *Big Book of Bugs*. It was now a **pupa**.

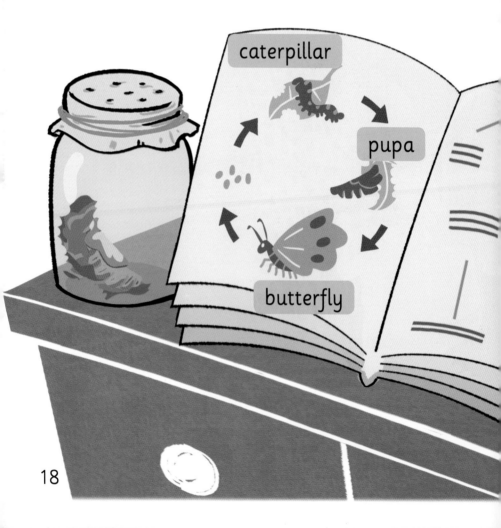

Doug carefully took the jam jars into the garden and put his bugs inside the bug hotel.

Doug looked at his bug hotel every day.
He saw the ladybird and the pupa inside.
There were lots of other bugs, too!

Doug was happy because there were lots of bugs in his bug hotel. But Sally did not like it!

"Doug, you know that I hate bugs!" she said.

One morning, Doug could see that the pupa was different.

"Look, Sally!" he said.

Doug and Sally watched a butterfly come from the pupa. The butterfly looked sad.

"Is it OK?" asked Sally.

"Yes, it is. Watch this!" said Doug.

After some time, the butterfly's **wings** started to open. They were beautiful. Doug and Sally watched the butterfly fly into the sky.

"I like butterflies. They are great!" said Sally.

"But butterflies are bugs, Sally!" said Doug.

The caterpillar was now a beautiful butterfly.

"Was that the caterpillar on the flowers?" said Sally. "That's fantastic!"

"And you like this bug!" said Doug. "That's fantastic, too!"

# Chapter 5 The birthday present

There were no bugs in Doug's bedroom, now. They were all in the bug hotel. Doug was sad.

"I want my bugs here!" said Doug.

"I know," said Sally.

It was Doug's birthday. Sally gave Doug a present. What was it?

Doug opened his present. There were
six stick insects in a big new tank! Doug was
very happy. It was a great present!

Doug and Sally looked at the *Big Book of Bugs*. Stick insects were easy pets.

Doug loved his bugs and now his big sister liked them, too.

"But I don't want them in my bedroom!" said Sally.

# Mini-dictionary

## Listen and read

**brick** (noun) A **brick** is a block in the shape of a rectangle. You use it to build walls.

**bug** (noun) Beetles, caterpillars, spiders and other small insects are called **bugs**.

**bug hotel** (noun) A **bug hotel** is a special place for insects to live in.

**cardboard** (noun) **Cardboard** is very thick paper that you can use to make boxes.

**flowerpot** (noun) A **flowerpot** is a container for you to grow flowers and plants in.

**jar** (noun) A **jar** is a round glass container that has a lid. You can keep food in it.

**log** (noun) A **log** is a thick piece of wood that someone has cut from a tree.

**pond** (noun) A **pond** is a small area of water which is big enough for fish to live in.

**pupa** (noun) A **pupa** is what a caterpillar turns into before it becomes a butterfly.

**recycling bin** (noun) A **recycling bin** is a container to put things in like paper or bottles so that we can use them again.

**rubber band** (noun) A **rubber band** is a thin circle of rubber that you put around things to keep them together.

**scared** (adjective) Someone who is **scared**, is afraid or worried.

**tank** (noun) A **tank** is a large glass container that you can keep things in.

**wing** (noun) An insect's **wings** are the parts of the body it uses to fly.

**worried** (adjective) If you are **worried**, you are unhappy because you think something is wrong.

**1** Look and order the story

**2** Listen and say

# Collins

Published by Collins
An imprint of HarperCollins*Publishers*
Westerhill Road
Bishopbriggs
Glasgow
G64 2QT

HarperCollins*Publishers*
1st Floor, Watermarque Building
Ringsend Road
Dublin 4
Ireland

William Collins' dream of knowledge for all began with the publication of his first book in 1819.

A self-educated mill worker, he not only enriched millions of lives, but also founded a flourishing publishing house. Today, staying true to this spirit, Collins books are packed with inspiration, innovation and practical expertise. They place you at the centre of a world of possibility and give you exactly what you need to explore it.

© HarperCollins*Publishers* Limited 2020

10 9 8 7 6 5 4 3 2

ISBN 978-0-00-839743-2

Collins® and COBUILD® are registered trademarks of HarperCollins*Publishers* Limited

www.collins.co.uk/elt

British Library Cataloguing in Publication Data

A catalogue record for this publication is available from the British Library.

Author: Jane Clarke
Illustrator: Esther P Cuadrado (Beehive)
Series editor: Rebecca Adlard
Commissioning editor: Zoë Clarke
Publishing manager: Lisa Todd
Product managers: Jennifer Hall and Caroline Green
In-house editor: Alma Puts Keren
Project manager: Emily Hooton
Editor: Matthew Hancock
Proofreaders: Natalie Murray and Michael Lamb
Cover designer: Kevin Robbins
Typesetter: 2Hoots Publishing Services Ltd
Audio produced by id audio, London
Reading guide author: Emma Wilkinson
Production controller: Rachel Weaver
Printed and bound by: GPS Group, Slovenia

Download the audio for this book and a reading guide for parents and teachers at www.collins.co.uk/839743